Captain AWESOME

☆ FOR PRESIDENT

By STAN KIRBY

Illustrated by GEORGE O'CONNOR

LITTLE SIMON

New York   London   Toronto   Sydney   New Delhi

LITTLE SIMON

An imprint of Simon & Schuster Children's Publishing Division • 1230 Avenue of the Americas, New York, New York 10020 • First Little Simon hardcover edition May 2018 • Copyright © 2018 by Simon & Schuster, Inc. • All rights reserved, including the right of reproduction in whole or in part in any form. • LITTLE SIMON is a registered trademark of Simon & Schuster, Inc., and associated colophon is a trademark of Simon & Schuster, Inc. • For information about special discounts for bulk purchases, please contact Simon & Schuster Special Sales at 1-866-506-1949 or business@simonandschuster.com. • The Simon & Schuster Speakers Bureau can bring authors to your live event. For more information or to book an event contact the Simon & Schuster Speakers Bureau at 1-866-248-3049 or visit our website at www.simonspeakers.com. • Designed by Jay Colvin. • The text of this book was set in Little Simon Gazette. • Manufactured in the United States of America 0418 FFG • 10 9 8 7 6 5 4 3 2 1

The Library of Congress has cataloged the paperback edition as follows:

Names: Kirby, Stan, author. | O'Connor, George, illustrator.

Title: Captain Awesome for president / by Stan Kirby ; illustrated by George O'Connor.

Description: First Little Simon paperback edition. | New York : Little Simon, 2018. | Series: Captain Awesome ; #20 | Summary: Eugene runs for second-grade class president against Meredith Mooney, but must find a way to prove he is best for the job without revealing either of their secret identities.

Identifiers: LCCN 2017048248 (print) | LCCN 2017058750 (eBook) |

ISBN 9781534420854 (eBook) | ISBN 9781534420830 (pbk) | ISBN 9781534420847 (hc)

Subjects: | CYAC: Superheroes—Fiction. | Politics, Practical—Fiction. | Elections—Fiction. | Schools—Fiction. | Friendship—Fiction. | BISAC: JUVENILE FICTION / Comics & Graphic Novels / Superheroes. | JUVENILE FICTION / Action & Adventure / General. | JUVENILE FICTION / Readers / Chapter Books.

Classification: LCC PZ7.K633529 (eBook) | LCC PZ7.K633529 Cagi 2018 (print) | DDC [Fic]—dc23

LC record available at https://lccn.loc.gov/2017048248

Table of Contents

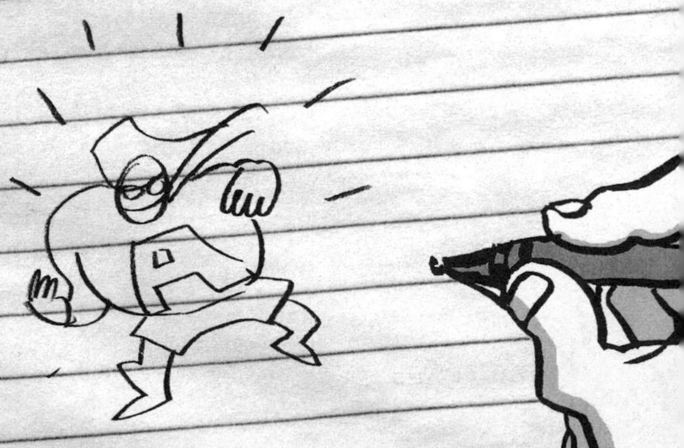

CHAPTER 1

Gymtastic!

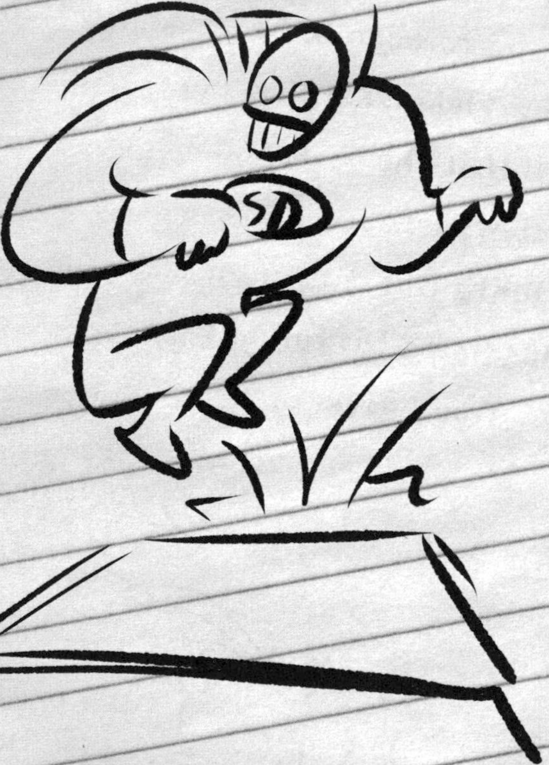

By
Eugene

Gym class could be a scary place for a superhero.

It was one place where their awesome powers could accidentally be revealed—if they jumped just a little *too* high, or ran just a little *too* fast. Just like that time in Super Dude No. 46 when Super Dude, the world's Dude-iest superhero, nearly revealed his secret identity as he fought the evil

Boing-Boing on his Trampoline of Jump Scares.

What's that you say? You've never heard of Super Dude, the star of the greatest comic books and graphic novels in the history of comic books and graphic novels? Super Dude and his colorful adventures were an inspiration to Eugene,

Sally, and Charlie—and the reason they formed the Sunnyview Superhero Squad.

"Be careful," Eugene whispered to Charlie and Sally as they entered the gym at Sunnyview Elementary.

"I know," Sally said. "Our superior skills might accidentally reveal that you're Captain Awesome and that I'm Supersonic Sal."

"And I'm Nacho Cheese Man!" Charlie announced as he pulled out a travel-size can of spray cheese.

"*Shhhhh!*" Sally and Eugene whispered at the same time. Sometimes their superfriend wasn't very

good at keeping his supersecret.

"We must be ever alert," Eugene said in his most heroic voice. "Gym can be as dangerous as any super-villain."

The whistle blew as Coach Bean ran onto the court. "Okay, dodgeballers, listen up! We'll split into two teams."

He pointed to Eugene. "Your captains will be McGillicudy and . . . Mooney." He pointed to Meredith, who was dressed in a bright pink dress and matching shoes and socks with a pink ribbon in her hair.

"Yes! I'll be the best captain!" Eugene said.

"Well, I'll be the *better* captain." Meredith stuck out her tongue.

The two captains stared at each other in a glare-down as Coach Bean picked the students for the teams.

Must. Keep. Eyes. Open, Eugene thought. He was determined not to blink first. But his eyes! They burned! Maybe this was all part of Little Miss Stinky Pinky's evil plan to win the game.

Eugene blinked.
Drat! Little Miss
Stinky Pinky may
have won this
glare-down, but
she wouldn't win
the dodgeball war.

Eugene rubbed
his eyes and surveyed
his team. There was Wilma
Eisner, Jane Romita, Howard Adams,
Sally, and . . .

GASP!
WAIT!
WHAT?

Where was Charlie? Eugene glanced at the other side of the court, where his best friend waved sadly from the other team.

CHAPTER 2

The UnFriender

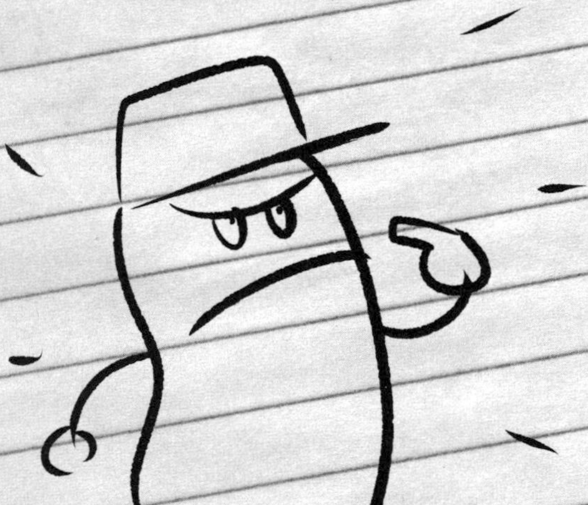

By Eugene

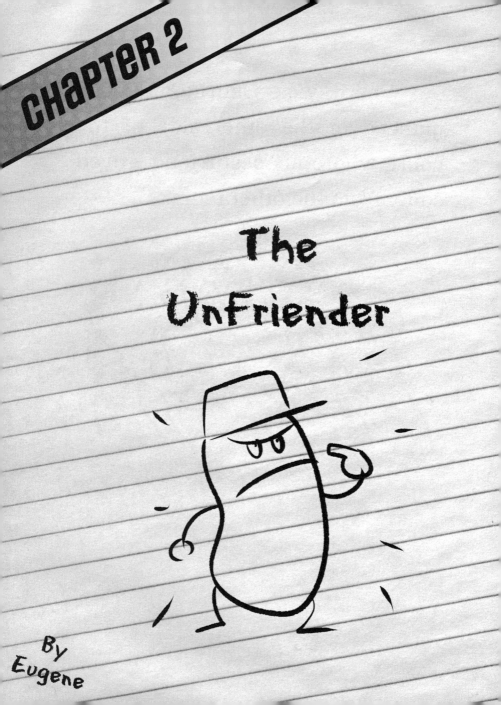

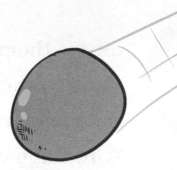

There could only be one reason why Charlie was put on Meredith's team. *Coach Bean's really the evil UnFriender, and his mission is to break up best friends!* Eugene thought frantically.

"All right, team, gather around," Eugene called. "Here's what we do. First, we're going to dodge all the balls that are thrown at us. Then, we're going to pick up the balls and

throw them back and
get the other team out!
Any questions?"

"Uh, Eugene,
we know how to
play dodgeball," Sally
pointed out.

Eugene's team ran onto the
court. Coach Bean tossed several
balls on the floor
between the two
teams. "Play ball!"

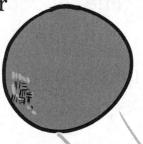

Both teams
raced for the balls
and threw them as

quickly as possible.
Sally threw an epic
toss at Meredith's
team.

BOING!
GIL DITKO!
OUT!

Meredith, Neal, Charlie, and Dara ran to the centerline, each holding a dodgeball. They threw the balls all at once!

BANG! BING!
JANE ROMITA!
HOWARD ADAMS!
OUT!

Eugene, Sally, and Wilma each picked up a ball and threw it back.

WHAMMO!
BAMMO!
DARA SIM!

CHARLIE THOMAS JONES! OUT!

Meredith picked up a ball as it bounced and threw it.

**PLOP!
WILMA EISNER!
OUT!**

It was Meredith and Neal against Sally and Eugene.

"All right, Pee-yew-gene, this is gonna be the end of you!" Meredith promised.

"Not a chance, Meredith!"

Eugene yelled back. "Victory will be my team's!"

Eugene and Sally took careful aim. They threw their balls. Meredith and Neal did the same.

All four balls hit all four kids at once. Everyone was out at the same time!

Coach Bean blew his whistle. "Game over," he yelled. "And it's a tie!"

A *tie! Ugh!* thought Eugene as
he watched Coach Bean pick up
the four dodgeballs and bag them.

This tie was all her fault. The
UnFriender might have weakened

his team this time, but the Sunny-view Superhero Squad would never let it happen again.

CHAPTER 3

A Presidential Announcement

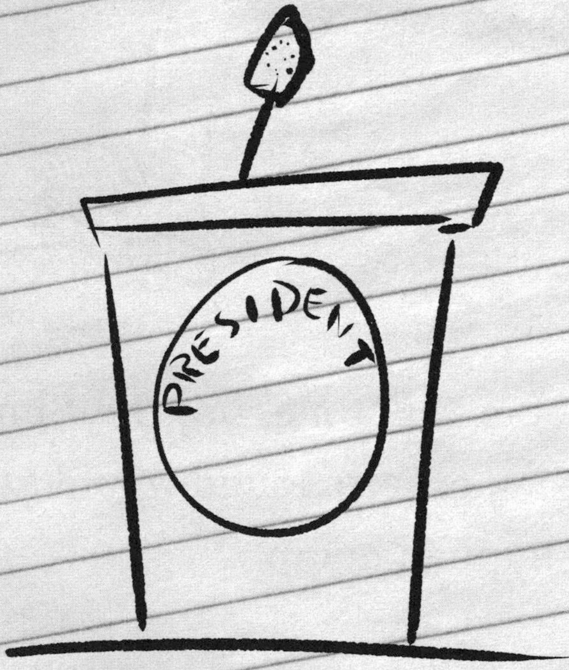
PRESIDENT

By Eugene

Eugene answered the final quiz question and put his pencil down just as Ms. Beasley dinged the time's-up bell on her desk. After she finished collecting all the papers, she cleared her throat.

"Class, if I can have your attention, please," Ms. Beasley said, "I have an announcement from our principal."

An announcement! Eugene was thrilled. *It could be any- thing,* he thought. *Another trip to the zoo! Early dis- missal! Ice- cream snack time!* Just the thought of a Triple Ripple brain freeze made Eugene shiver with excitement.

"Every grade in Sunnyview Elementary is going to elect their own class president," she said, "and every student is welcome to partici- pate and campaign!"

The class gasped.

"Just think," Ms. Beasley said, "in a country where anyone can grow up to be president, here at

Sunnyview Elementary, you don't even have to wait to grow up!"

Then Ms. Beasley explained the rules. Each candidate had to come up with a slogan and make posters. Then they would hit the campaign trail and visit each second-grade classroom to try to convince the classes to vote for them.

All the students started chatting excitedly.

"YES!" Eugene threw his hands into the air and turned to Charlie. "This will be more exciting than the time Super Dude

defeated the Big Bad Boredom
Brothers in Super Dude number
seventeen."

"More exciting than Double Cheese Friday," Charlie said thoughtfully.

"Are you guys going to run?" Eugene asked his two friends.

"I'd love to," Sally said, "but I'm busy with soccer and gymnastics and piano."

"I'm out," Charlie said. "It would inter-fere with Cheese Craft."

"Cheese Craft?" asked Eugene and Sally.

"It's just the greatest video game ever," Charlie said. "I build worlds out of cheese, and then I play Cheesy Stevie and go hunting for yummy cheese balls that give me power."

"Are *you* going to run?" Sally asked Eugene.

"Is spandex itchy?!" Eugene cried. "Being president would be like being a school superhero, but without a mask!"

"We should come up with some ideas for your campaign, then," Sally said. "We'll have to convince a lot of kids to vote for you."

"Let's meet at the Sunnyview Superhero Squad headquarters after school," Eugene suggested.

"Perfect!" Charlie said. "Today is my day off from Cheese Craft!"

CHAPTER 4

Brainstorming Blitz

By
Eugene

Who wants chocolate chip cookies?" Mrs. McGillicudy asked as Eugene, Charlie, and Sally walked into the kitchen. "Can't brainstorm without a full brain!"

"Thanks, Mom!" Eugene said. "This is just how I think Cookie Blaster smelled in the Super Dude Summer BBQ Spectacular number one."

The trio grabbed handfuls of

freshly baked treats and raced into the backyard. Their headquarters was also Eugene's tree house. They climbed the tree house ladder— which was surprisingly hard to do with a handful of freshly baked treats.

Once they finally did make it safely to the top, Sally called the meeting to order. "So, what's first?" she asked.

"I vote that Eugene's mom makes the best chocolate chip cookies," Charlie said. "There's only one thing missing." He blasted a squirt

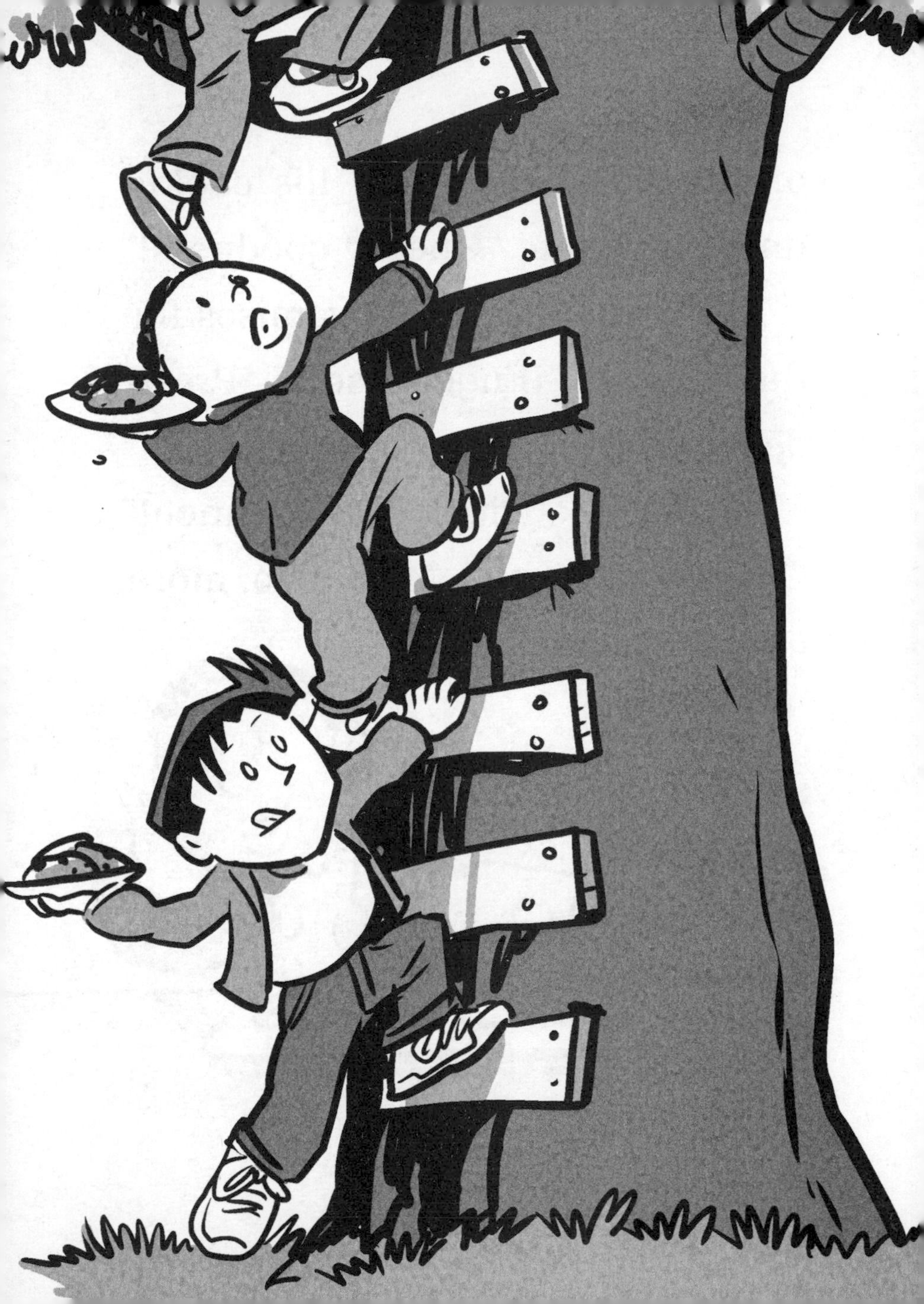

of canned cheese onto his cookie and took a bite. "Cheesy goodness!"

"I need some cool promises for the election," Eugene said. "Presidents always make promises."

"Cheese with every lunch!" Charlie suggested. "And also, more cheese at snack time!"

"I think we should have more running in the halls," Sally offered. "Kids could get to recess faster."

"Or lunch," Charlie agreed.

"I think no quizzes," Eugene said. "And no tests, either! And

somebody should apologize for all the tests so far!"

"I've got one," Charlie said. "Every day is a Get Out Early Day!"

"How about five more minutes of recess if we do well on a quiz?" Sally suggested.

"How about a Superhero Day!" Eugene said.

"That's a great idea!" Sally agreed. "Everyone can dress up like their favorite superhero! We could all go as Super Dude!"

"That would be great!" Eugene said. "It'd be just like that time in

Super Dude number nine, when Super Dude teamed up with the Dude Twins to fight the Triple Triplets."

"You'll still need a slogan. 'Vote for the Cheesiest President Ever!'" Charlie suggested.

"'The Speedy President!'" Sally said.

Eugene cried out. "Wait, I've got it! 'An awesome president for an awesome school!'"

CHAPTER 5

The Tiebreaker

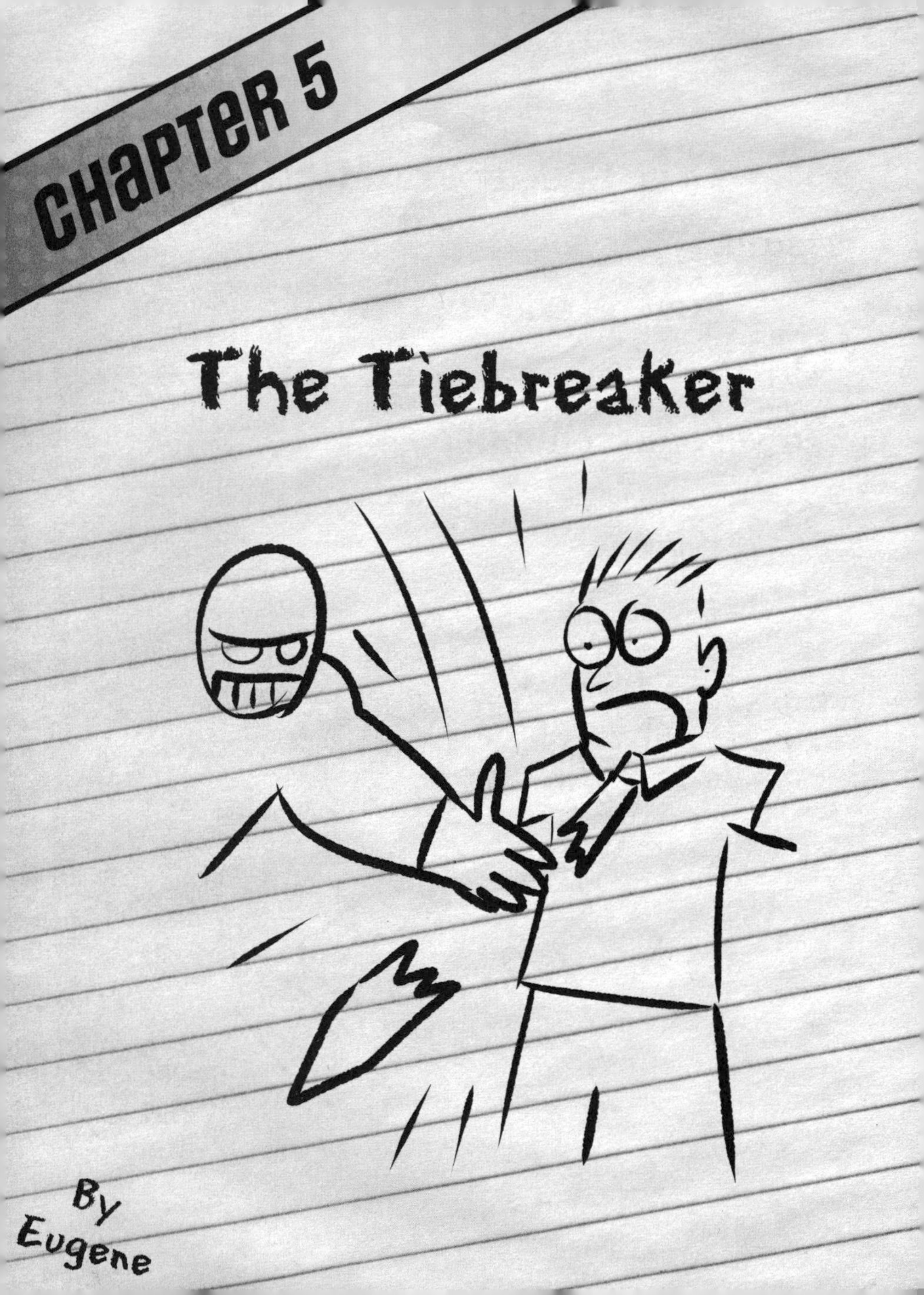

By Eugene

Good morning, Terrible Trio," Meredith said as Eugene, Charlie, and Sally entered school the next morning. "So, I just wanted to let you know that I've decided to *let* you vote for me. No need to thank me."

"Why would we vote for you?" Charlie asked.

"Because I'm running for queen," Meredith replied.

"Don't you mean *president*?" Sally asked.

"Only if you spell it *q-u-e-e-n*," Meredith replied.

"Well, I'm running for *p-r-e-z*..." Eugene trailed off as he tried to puzzle out the spelling.

"*P-r-e-s-i-d-e-n-t*, president," Sally helpfully finished. "We're on our way to sign Eugene up."

Meredith gagged. "Really? Looks like we found our tiebreaker for yesterday's dodgeball game,

Eugerm. Whoever wins the election wins the tiebreaker. And that will, of course, be me!" She looked down the hallway. "And we can start . . . NOW!"

Meredith took off down the hall.

Eugene chased after her. There was no time to change into his Captain Awesome suit for this patriotic race.

As they sped around a corner, Eugene almost ran into the Hot Lava

Bucket the janitor used to burn the bathroom floor clean. The lava bubbled and boiled in the metal bucket. Eugene leaped over it.

The door to the Basement of Fear was open. Eugene quickly swerved to the side. *That was a close one*, he thought. *Who knows what's down there?!*

Meredith was not far ahead now. Eugene had a chance. He used his Awesome-Powers. His feet sped up even faster.

Just then the pink ribbon fluttered out of Meredith's hair. It flew into Eugene's face. "Argh!" he cried out. "I can't see!"

Eugene yanked the ribbon off
himself just as
his feet slid out
from under him.

"Aaah!" Eugene slid toward his
classroom on his stomach.

Sometime during the night, Super
Waximina must have broken into

the school to spill her superslippery liquid Wax of Doom on the floor.

Ms. Beasley stood in the doorway, holding a clipboard with the sign-up sheet. Meredith came to a sudden stop.

"Look out!" Eugene cried. He crashed into Meredith, and she fell on top of him. "Another tie!" he groaned.

Ms. Beasley helped her students up. "How many times do I have to tell you kids? You're not allowed to run in the hall!" She held out the clipboard. "However, you *are* allowed to run for class president. Do you want to sign up?"

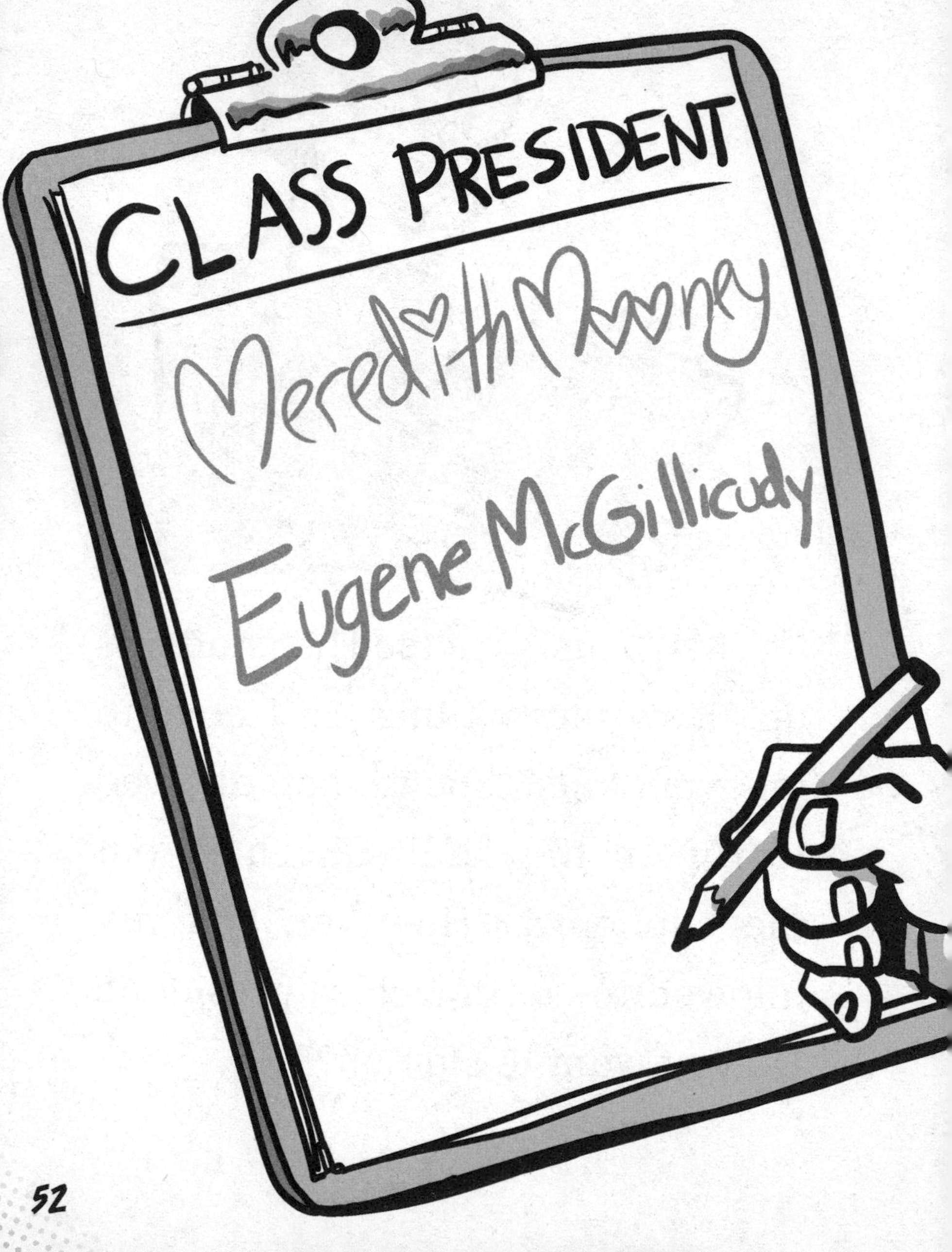
CLASS PRESIDENT
Meredith Mooney
Eugene McGillicudy

"You bet I do, Ms. Beasley," Meredith said.

"Me too," Eugene said, and signed his name.

"And I'm running too!" Dara Sim exclaimed.

"Excellent!" Ms. Beasley said. "Good luck to you all."

Now this is what I call a race! thought Eugene excitedly.

CHAPTER 6

All Hail the Queen

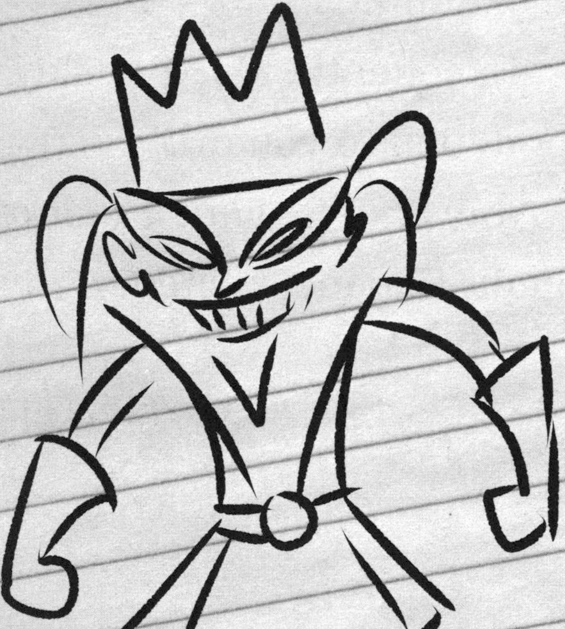

By
Eugene

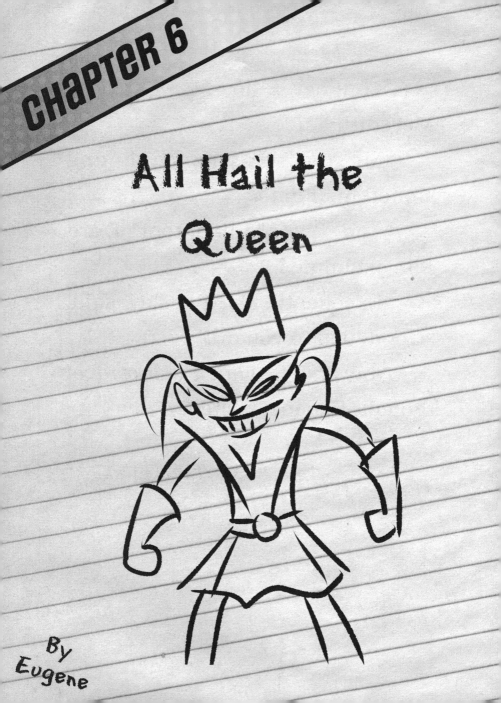

The three friends met at school bright and early the next morning to hang all the posters Eugene had made overnight. Sally complimented his super art. But Charlie thought it wasn't cheesy enough. He added one or two quick squirts from his trusty can to brighten up a few posters while the others worked farther down the hall.

The school bell rang just as they finished hanging the last poster at the entrance to the Basement of Fear. Perfect timing!

But as Eugene was about to follow Sally and Charlie into their classroom, Ms. Beasley blocked him. "Stop right there," she said.

Uh-oh! If his teacher hadn't had her morning coffee yet, she sometimes morphed into the dreaded supervillain . . . Miss Beastly!

"You're supposed to be campaigning in Mrs. Duncan's class," his teacher continued.

Oops! Eugene turned right around and sprinted back down the hall.

"No running!" Ms. Beasley called out after him.

Eugene arrived in time to join Meredith and Dara Sim at the front of Mrs. Duncan's second-grade

CLASS PRESID

class. Collin Boyle was also there.

"Okay, class. Now we're going to hear from the students who are running for second-grade president," Mrs. Duncan explained. "They're going to make short speeches and introduce themselves."

Eugene stared silently at the

twenty-eight faces staring back at him. *SPEECHES? Oh, man! We have to make speeches?! In front of people?!*

Dara Sim went first. Eugene couldn't hear what she was saying because he was too distracted by the deafening sound of his pounding heart.

Was Super Dude this nervous when he made a speech about his new Super Dude Superhero Underwear at the superhero costume convention in

Super Dude No. 77? Eugene tried to calm himself down. *No! He just talked about its superstretchiness!*

Eugene looked down. *Maybe I should talk about my underwear too?*

It felt like a thousand butterflies were riding a roller coaster in

Eugene's stomach. But then he had a great idea. Eugene snuck into the hallway as Dara finished.

"Okay, Eugene. You're next," Mrs. Duncan said. "Eugene?"

"Looks like Eugerm decided to run away," Meredith said, and laughed.

The classroom door flung open!

"Hold, pink one!" a heroic voice called out. "Eugene asked me to speak to the class for him."

"Ah . . . you must be Captain . . . Possum?" Mrs. Duncan said. "Ms. Beasley's told me a lot about you. A *whole lot.*"

"The name is Awesome," Captain Awesome corrected. "As in, 'It's *awesome* to meet you, ma'am.'"

Captain Awesome stepped in front of Meredith. She crossed her arms and stuck out her tongue.

"Students! Lend me your ears!"

There were no nervous butterflies doing ninja kicks in Captain
Awesome's stomach. "If you vote
for Eugene McGillicudy for president, he'll make sure none of your
teachers are supervillains! He will

outlaw
any home-
work
that
would
melt your
brain,
and he'll
make sure
all food
served in the cafeteria isn't really
an alien body snatcher. Thank you."
Captain Awesome turned to leave,
then remembered to add, "Oh, and
he'll be an *awesome* president!"

The kids clapped as Captain Awesome raced from the room so fast, Meredith didn't even have time to stick out her tongue again.

"Um, well, that was inspiring," Mrs. Duncan said. "Now it's your turn, Meredith."

Eugene slipped back into the room as Meredith started her speech.

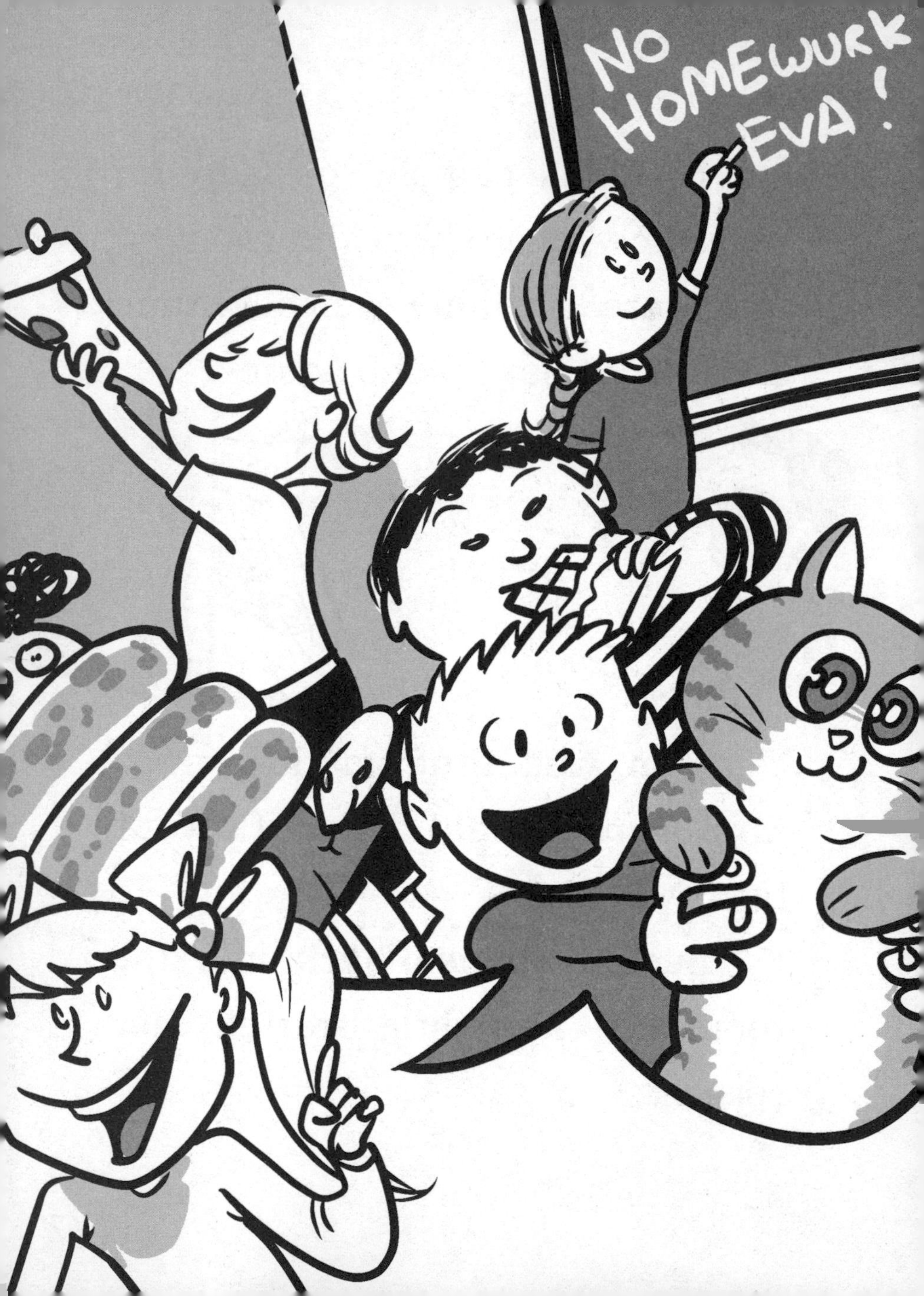
NO HOMEWURK EVA!

"If you vote for me," Meredith began, "I promise the cafeteria will only serve pizza, hot dogs, potato chips, and any food that's dipped in chocolate. There will be less homework on Wednesdays and no homework on Mondays, Tuesdays, Thursdays, and Fridays. Every day will be Bring Your Pet to School Day, and every third Tuesday, the teachers will have to stay home and we'll run the school. Thank you."

Meredith bowed and the class burst into cheers and happy shouts. Eugene felt the butterflies come

back. Winning wasn't going to be as easy as he thought, especially if Meredith was making crazy promises.

"Are you sure it's a good idea to promise all those things, Meredith?" Eugene asked quietly. "I doubt the school will let you do any of that."

"By the time everyone realizes

that, it'll be too late. They'll have already voted for me, and I'll be their new queen," Meredith whispered back.

"Don't you mean president?" Eugene asked.

"No, Eugerm," Meredith said, "I do not."

CHAPTER 7

Sabotage!

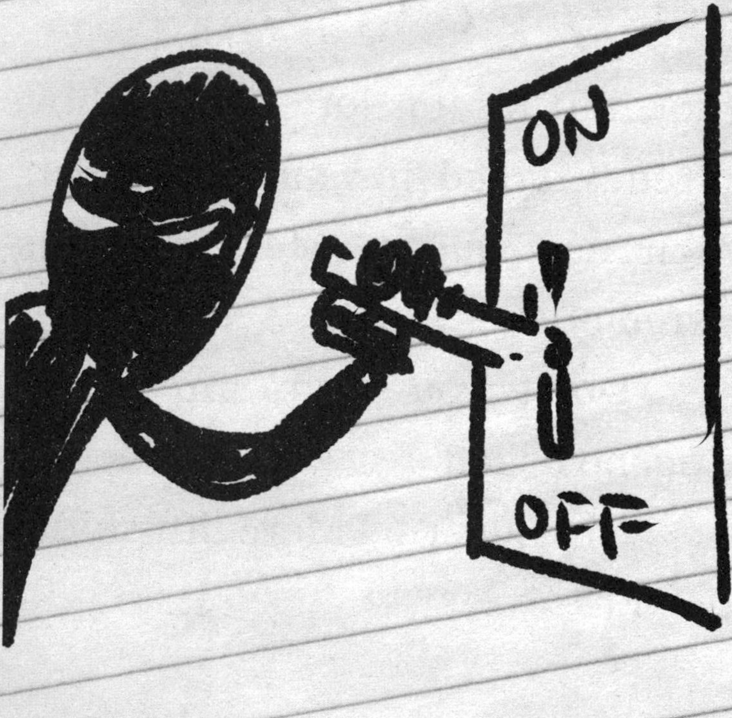
ON
OFF

By
Eugene

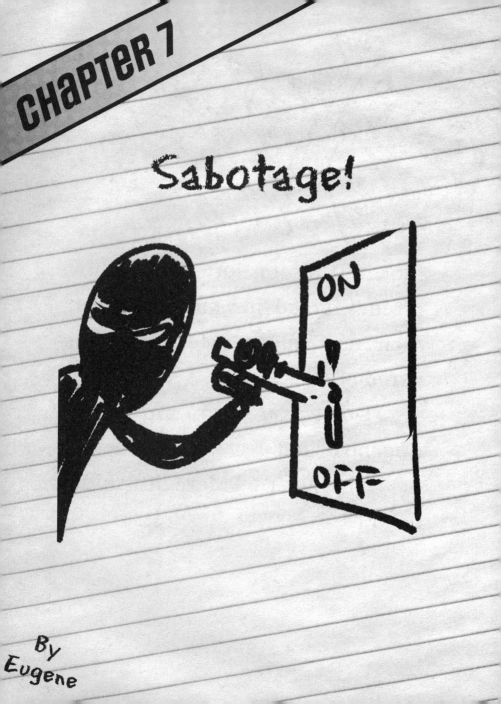

The rest of the week went by faster than Super Turbo's Turbomobile on a rocket. Eugene, Meredith, Dara, and Collin hung more posters, visited more second-grade classrooms, shook hands, and continued making big promises. With each classroom visit, Eugene became more and more comfortable. . . . But then Friday came.

Usually Friday was the best day of the week that didn't start with the letter *S*. But not this week. The candidates were set to make their final speeches . . .

IN FRONT OF THE WHOLE SECOND GRADE!

Eugene, Meredith, Collin, and

Dara sat backstage in the school auditorium with the rest of the candidates from other grades, waiting for their turn to speak. This time, it felt like the butterflies in Eugene's stomach had invited all their cousins to join them.

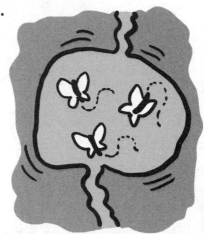

The principal called Meredith's name. It was speech time.

Meredith stepped up to the podium. Then she put on a smile

so wide that Eugene thought she might break her face.

"I'm sure all of you already know who I am," Meredith began. "If you've been living under a rock, then my name's Meredith Mooney. When you elect me to be your queen— I mean, *president*"—Meredith tried not to chuckle—"I promise to give every single one of you

everything you want forever and
ever. The end."

The auditorium erupted in
loud applause as Meredith led the
students in a cheer of "Don't be
loony! Vote for Meredith Mooney!"

"It's catchy because it *rhymes*," Charlie said from the audience.

But the teachers didn't find it so funny.

Meredith turned to walk away, but then she paused when she saw Ms. Beasley frowning at her. She turned back to the audience quickly.

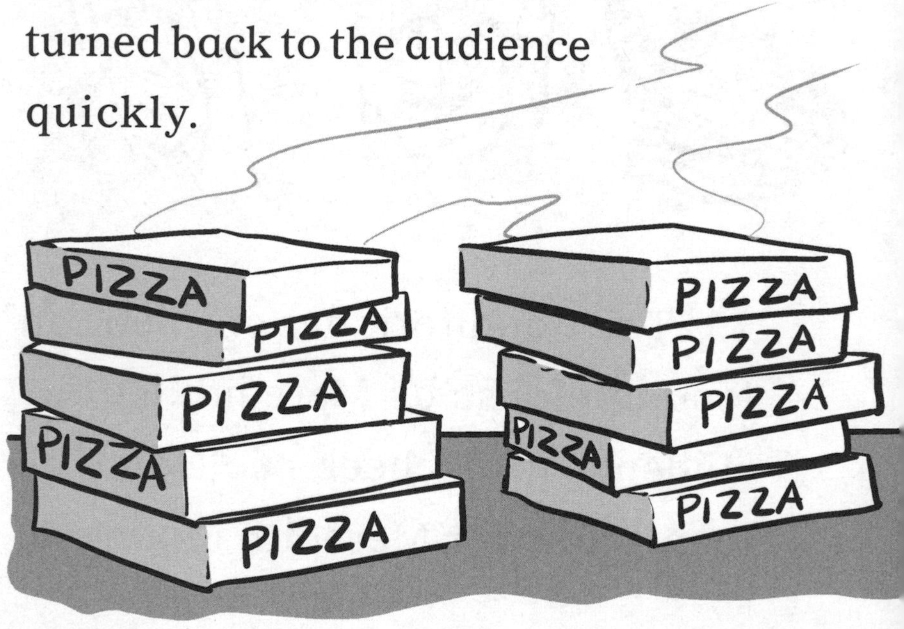
PIZZA
PIZZA
PIZZA
PIZZA
PIZZA
PIZZA
PIZZA
PIZZA
PIZZA
PIZZA

"And I'll also, oh, I don't know, have a bake sale or something to raise money for the school and we can have a pizza party or whatever."

Meredith blew a single kiss and skipped off the stage. The cheers were so loud, they shook dust from the lights overhead.

Collin went next. Eugene wasn't exactly sure what he even said because the cheers for Meredith were still so loud.

Next came Dara Sim. The kids in the audience were tired of shouting Meredith's name and sat in bored silence once more.

"I promise to work with the teachers to make class better for everyone," Dara said. "I have a plan that lets kids earn a Homework Skip Pass by keeping their grades up. I also have an idea that would let us raise extra money to buy tablets for the classrooms."

Hushed whispers passed through the crowd.

"YAWN!" Meredith called out.

"To me, a president is supposed to do what's right, help people who need it, and make people's lives better," Dara finished. "And that's what I'd like to do for this school."

Wow, that was really good, thought Eugene. *But now I need to focus on beating Meredith. How can I do that if everyone believes all that junk she's promising? I'd need to do something crazy . . . like tell everyone she's really a supervillain.*

Eugene's heart skipped. "That's brilliant!" he cried. "No one would vote for a supervillain!" Filled with hope, Eugene rushed onto the stage before the principal even said his name. He was ready to make the shortest speech in election history. It was only going to be six words. . . .

MEREDITH IS REALLY LITTLE MISS STINKY PINKY!

But suddenly the lights went out.

CHAPTER 8

Lights Out

BY
Eugene

Everyone, stay calm and remain seated," Ms. Beasley called out. "There's no reason to panic."

"Your future queen is in the dark, and you think there's no reason to panic?!" Meredith yelled.

Is someone sabotaging my speech? Eugene wondered as he stumbled into his backpack. *Which of my archenemies could it be? Whoever it is, they're gonna be* sorry they messed with . . . **CAPTAIN AWESOME!**

BACKPACK! Uh, it's some-where. It is kinda dark.

ZIPPER! Wait. . . . Where's the zipper again?

COSTUME! Nope. That's an old sock. Try again.

COSTUME! Nailed it! **MI-TEE!**

Eugene pulled out the mini-flashlight he kept in his backpack just in case a supervillain ever tried to steal the sun. He made his way to Charlie and Sally, who had pulled on their own costumes and rushed toward the stage to help their friend. The trio snuck over to the auditorium door.

"One flick of the light switch, and we'll send evil

scrambling back to the shadows," Captain Awesome said.

FLICK!
FLICK!
FLICK?
FLICK!
FLICK! FLICK! FLICK!
FLICK! FLICK!

"The light switch isn't working!" Captain Awesome gasped.

"We should try the circuit breakers," Supersonic Sal suggested.

"The how-a-ma-what?" Nacho Cheese Man asked.

"The *circuit breakers*. They're the switches that control the electricity going into the whole building," Supersonic Sal explained. "Our house is old, and my dad has to go and fix ours in the basement all the time."

"They do what-a-ma-who to where?" Nacho Cheese Man said.

"Just lead the way, Sal," Captain Awesome said.

Luckily, these circuit breakers weren't in the Basement of Fear. They were in a closet at the top of the auditorium stairs. Supersonic Sal opened a small panel door to reveal the numerous breaker switches.

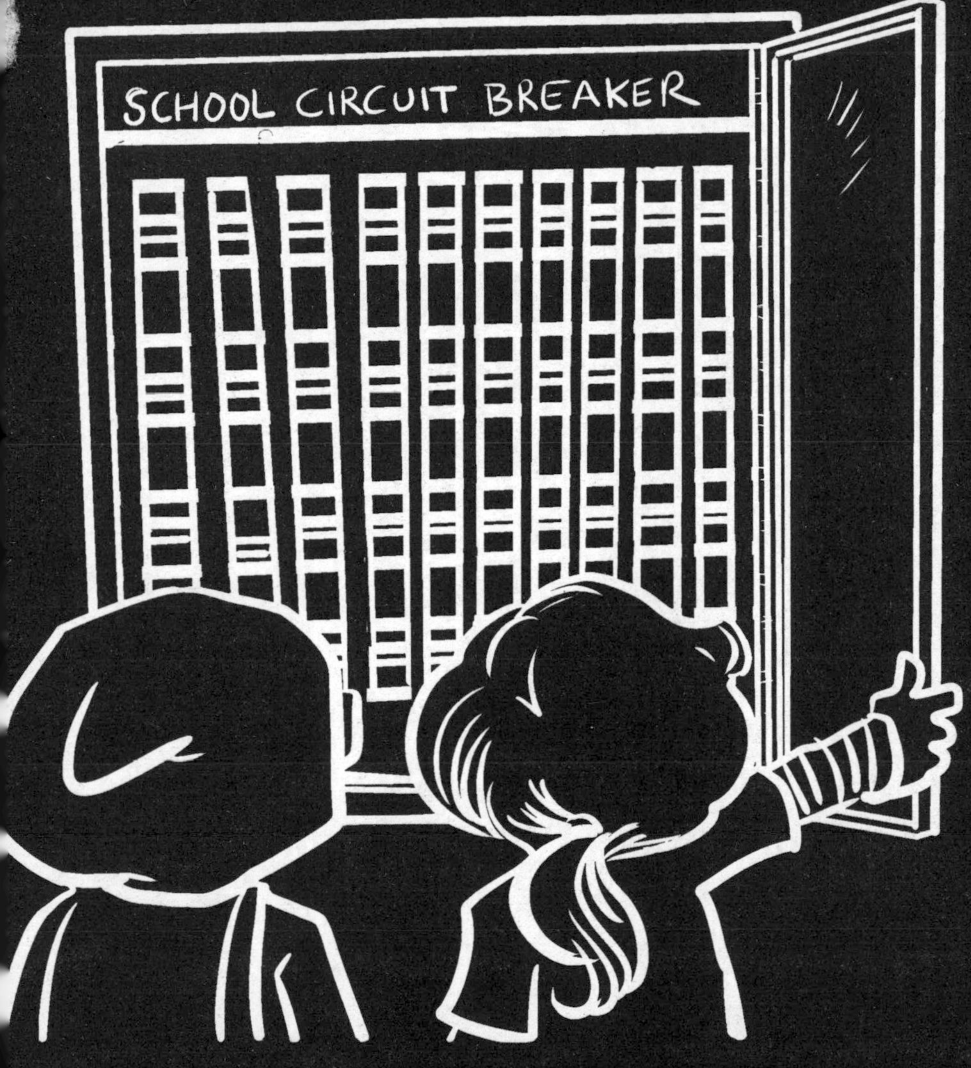
SCHOOL CIRCUIT BREAKER

"Should I spray them with some cheese?" Nacho Cheese Man asked.

"No! Cheese and electricity do *not* mix," Supersonic Sal said. She scanned the switches with the flashlight. "I just have to figure out which is the right switch to turn the lights back on. . . ."

"What happens if you're wrong?" Captain Awesome tried not to sound too nervous. "Will we be blasted into space and have to live on the planet Astrotopia forever?!"

"This is it!" Supersonic Sal reached out for the switch.

Nacho Cheese Man gulped! Captain Awesome closed his eyes!

FLIP!

FLICKER! FLICKER!

"Aaaaaah! We're being blasted to Astrotopia!" Nacho Cheese Man yelled.

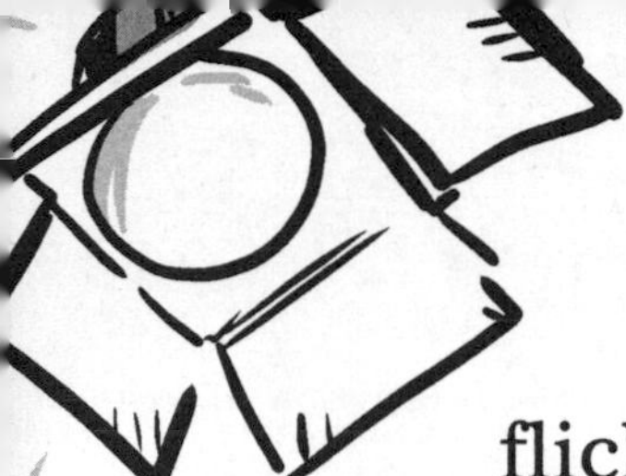

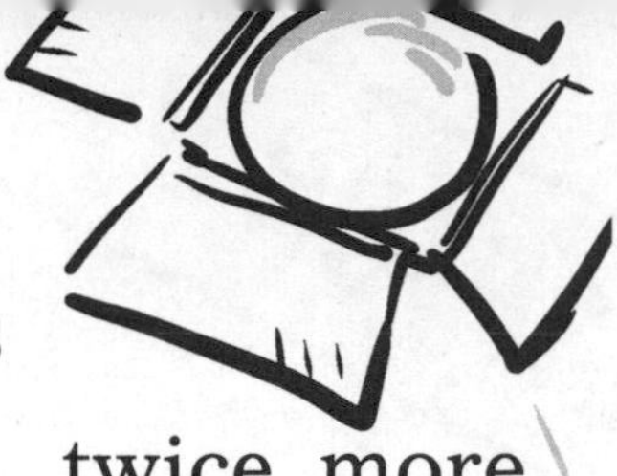

The lights flickered once, twice more, then came back on. It was the right switch!

"Hey, what are you kids doing back here?" It was the janitor, aka ***THE PERILOUS PLUNGER!***

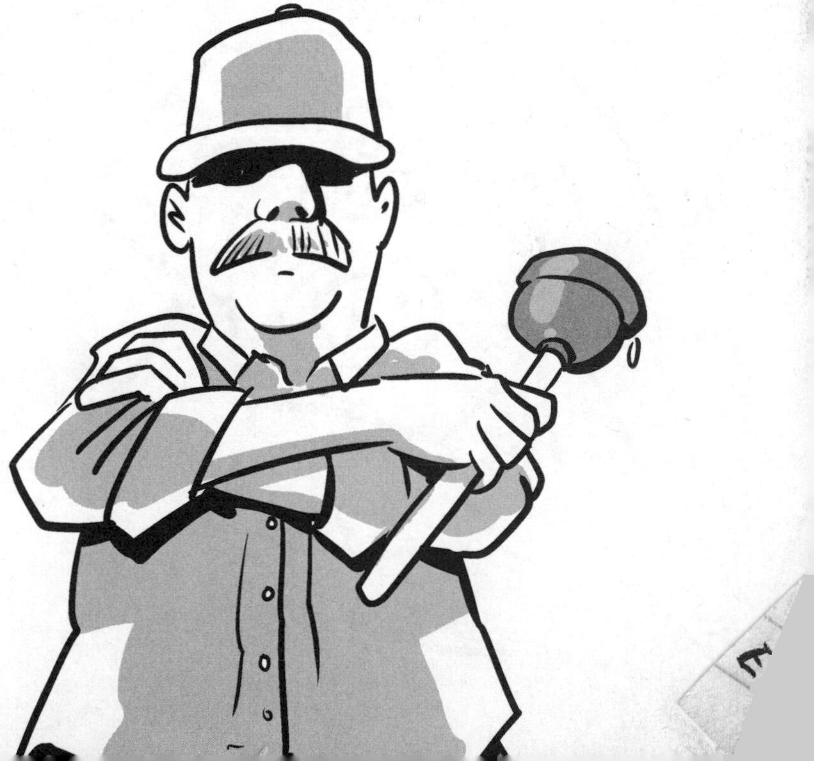

CHAPTER 9

Making a Difference

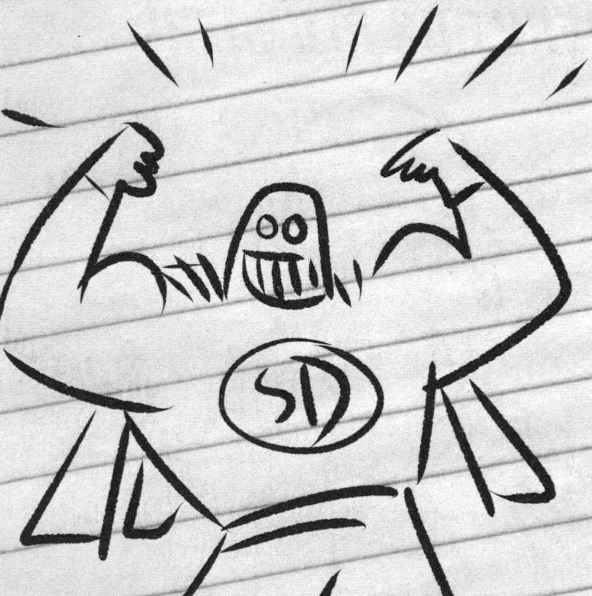
SD

By
ene

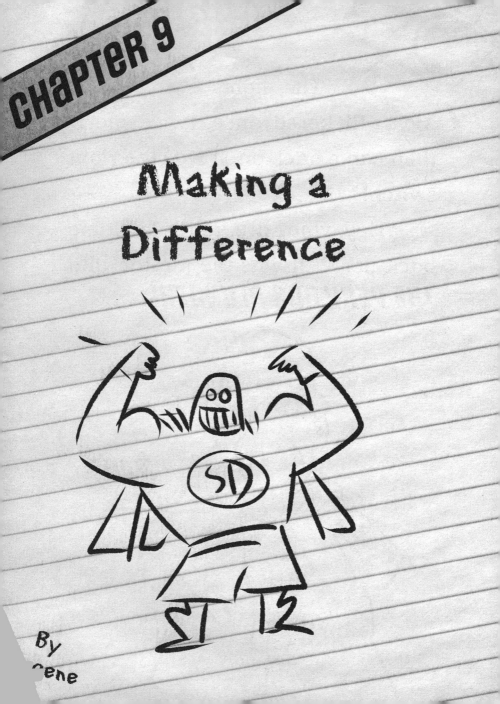

I get stuck plunging the boys' room for *one minute*, and I come back to utter chaos," the Perilous Plunger complained as he angrily shook his Atomic Plunger.

"Hey! Watch where you're pointing that weapon!" cried Supersonic Sal.

Nacho Cheese Man quickly stepped in. "What she means to say is, we're sorry, Your Smelliness. But it was our duty to help our school and defeat the Darkness."

Captain Awesome was very impressed by Nacho Cheese Man's sudden diplomacy.

"Yeah, well, I guess there's no harm done," admitted the janitor. "But you guys better get back over

to the rest of the assembly before one of the teachers catches you out of your seats!"

Eugene stared down at the crowd. *GULP!*

Remember, all you've got to do is tell everyone that Meredith is really Little Miss Stinky Pinky, and she'll lose for sure! Eugene reminded himself as he walked to the podium.

"I hope he's gonna give us all

rocket ships," Gil Ditko whispered loudly to Jake Story.

Eugene took a deep breath. It was time to tell everyone the truth about Meredith. But strangely, it wasn't Meredith's words that kept ringing in Eugene's head. It was Dara's. *A president is supposed to do what's right, help people who*

need it, and make people's lives better.

It reminded him of what Super Dude told his new sidekick, Li'l Super Duper Dude, in Super Dude No. 129: *Being able to fly isn't what makes us heroes. We're heroes because we make a difference when no one else can.*

"Um . . . I know a lot of you are waiting for me to make some crazy promises," Eugene began.

"I want a rocket!" Gil Ditko yelled from his seat.

"Well, that's the thing. I can't give you a rocket," Eugene continued. "I can only *tell* you

that. I can also tell you that I'll give everyone everything they want plus infinity forever, but I really can't give anyone that, either. No one can." Eugene felt a lump form in his throat. "Look, you can vote for someone who will make you crazy promises, or you can vote for someone who has a real plan to help this school. I want to do what's right and help people. That's why I think you should vote for . . . Dara Sim. Thank you."

Eugene walked off the stage to total silence except for the echoing laughter of Meredith.

"HA! HA! HA! HA! Nice speech, Eugerm!" she yelled.

"What just happened?" Charlie
asked Eugene when the assembly
was over.

"I really liked Dara's speech."
Eugene shrugged.

"Well, I think that was very brave," said Sally.

Eugene smiled.

CHAPTER 10

A True Leader

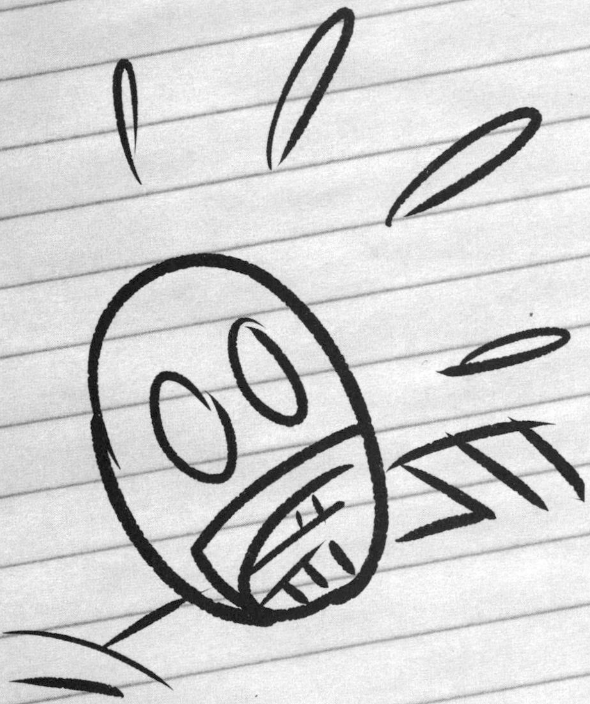

By
Eugene

The next day, Eugene arrived at school feeling better than he had in days. Until he encountered Meredith in full meltdown mode.

"WHAT DO YOU MEAN I LOST?!" Meredith shouted. "THAT'S NOT POSSIBLE! I'M THE QUEEN! ME! ME! MEREDITH! RECOUNT! I DEMAND A RECOUNT!"

Eugene was stunned! If Meredith lost, could that mean . . . ?

"I WON?!" Eugene gasped.

"Nope. Dara did," Charlie said.

Eugene's heart sank for a moment, but then he realized it was awesome that Dara had won. She was the best kid for the job.

"Everyone did a great job, and I'm proud of you all. You should be proud too," Ms. Beasley said.

Meredith folded her arms and plopped down in her chair. "I

don't want to be proud. I want to be QUEEN!"

Eugene shook Dara's hand. "You made a great speech. You deserved to win."

"Thanks, Eugene," Dara replied. "And thanks for what you said during your speech. It was pretty cool."

"We may only be second graders, but we weren't born yesterday," Ellen Moore said.

"It was fun to cheer for those crazy things Meredith promised, but she'd need a fairy wand to make them all come true."

"DARA! DARA! DARA!" the kids in class started to chant. Meredith was the only one not chanting.

"Maybe you could go talk to her?" Dara suggested.

"Me?! No way!" Eugene exclaimed.

"I don't know if you can say no to the *president*," Sally said.

Eugene gritted his teeth and walked very, very slowly over to Meredith's seat.

"I think you did a great job," he told her.

"Not good enough." Meredith sighed.

"Maybe next year we can try again. We could even come up with a real plan like Dara did," Eugene suggested hopefully.

Eugene braced himself for what Meredith

was going to say back. But instead she nodded. "Yeah. Maybe," she said. And then quickly mumbled, "And-youdidagood-jobtooIguess."

Eugene and Meredith shook hands.

Dara definitely deserves to be president. She must be a great president if she

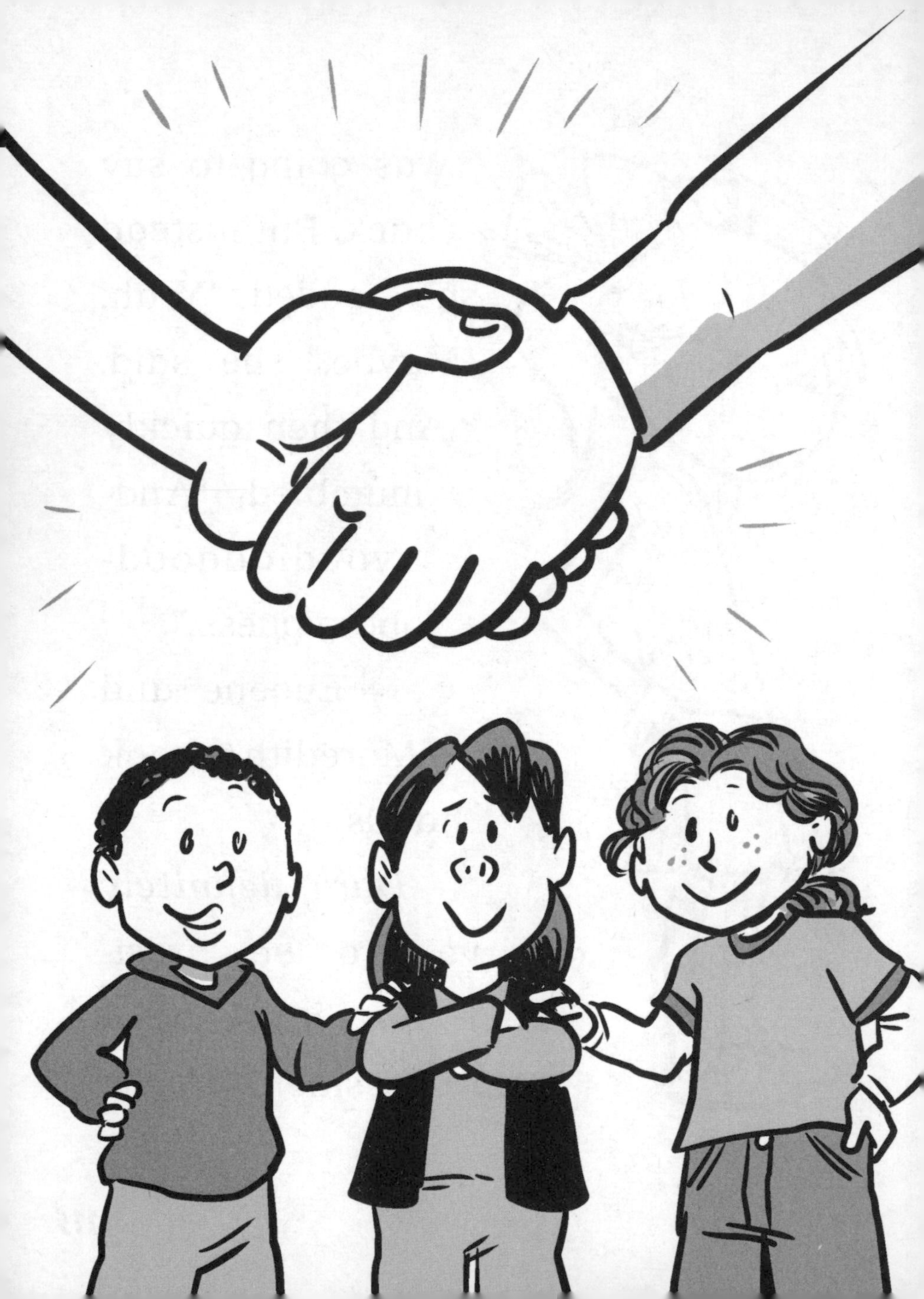

got Meredith and me to be nice to each other! Eugene thought. And that was pretty . . .

MI-TEE!

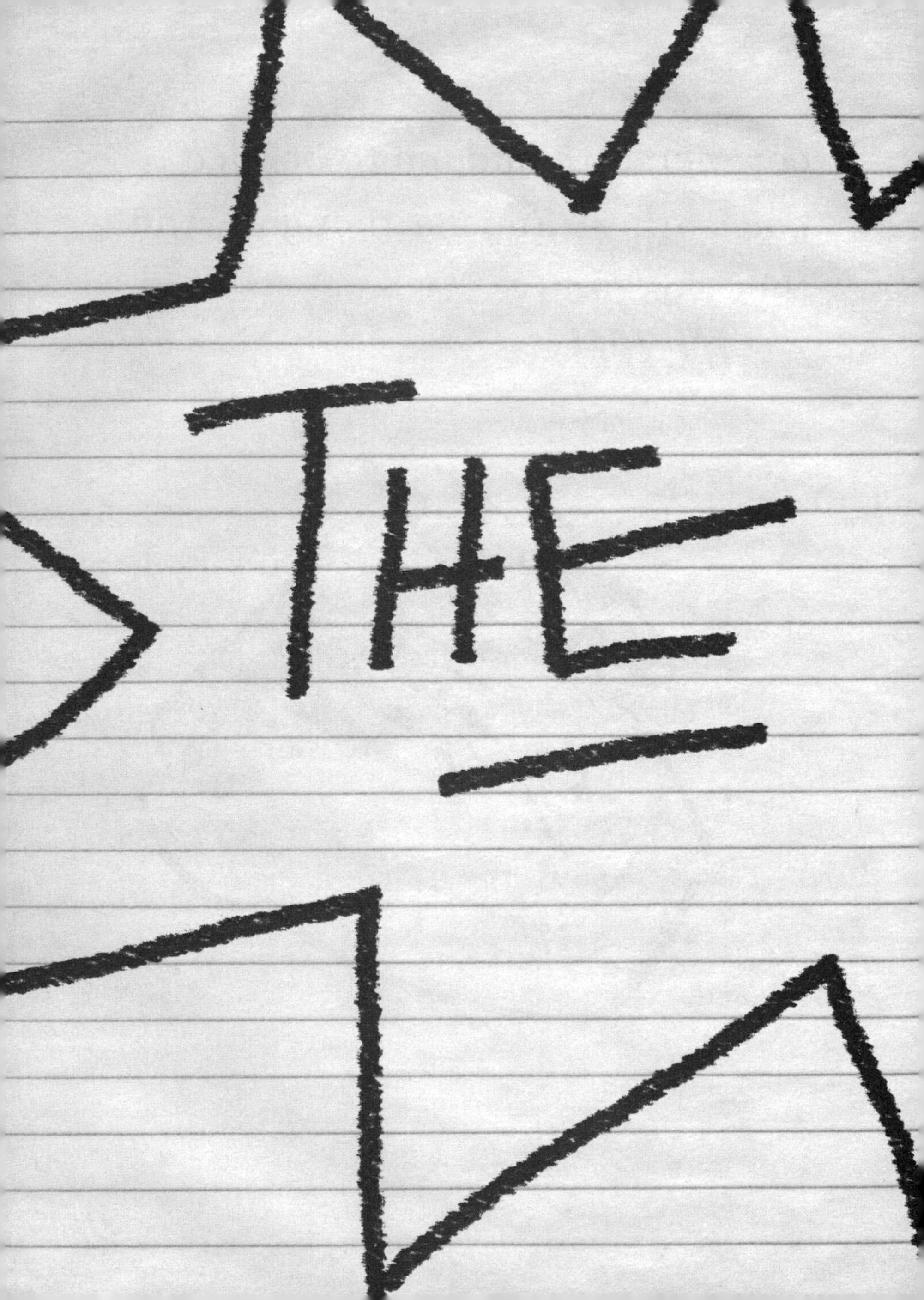
THE

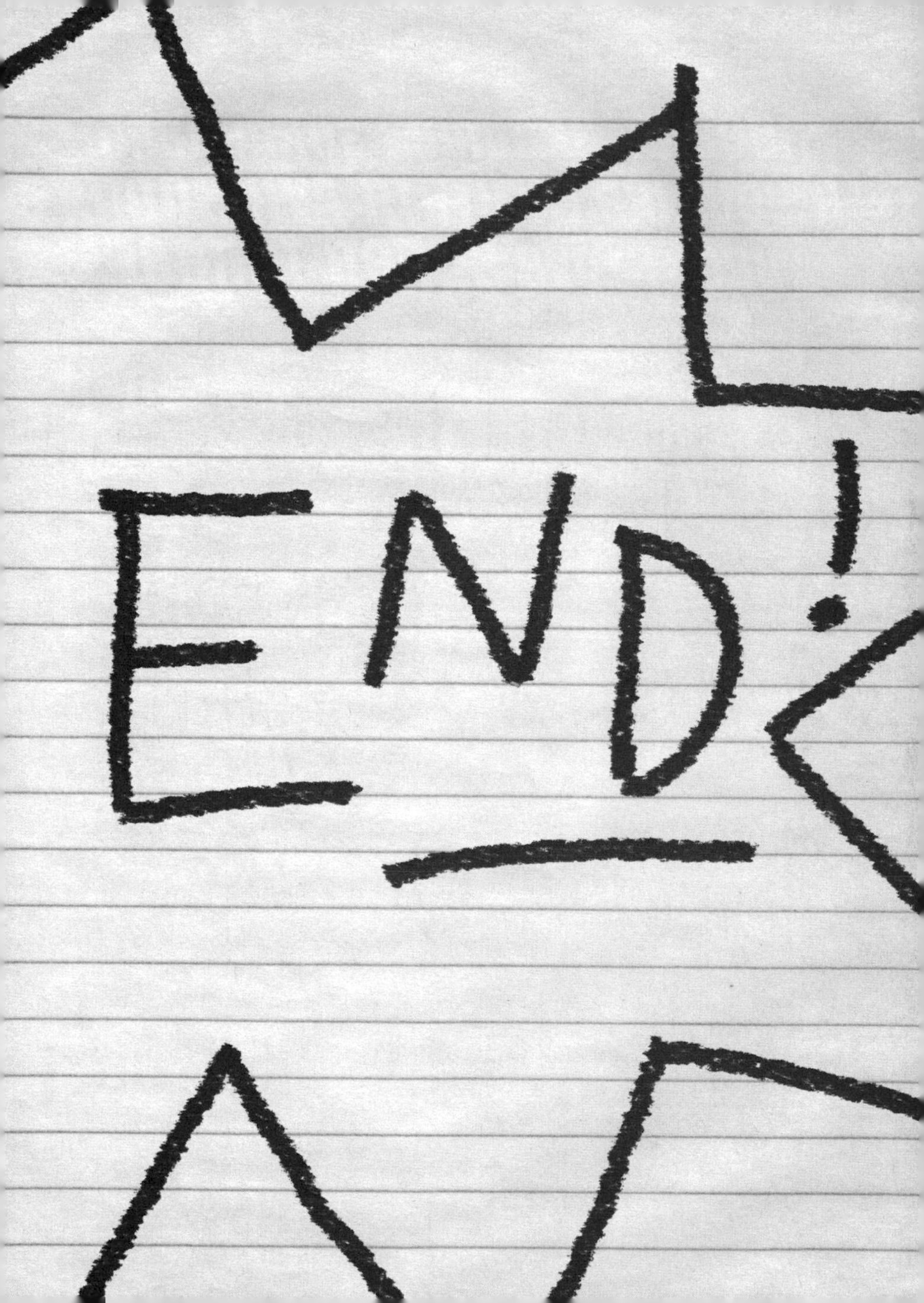
END!

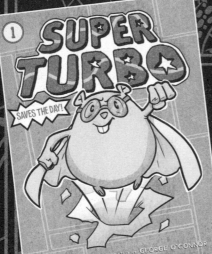

MI-TEE!

Visit
CaptainAwesomeBooks.com
for completely awesome
activities, excerpts,
tips from Turbo, and
the series trailer!

Little
Simon

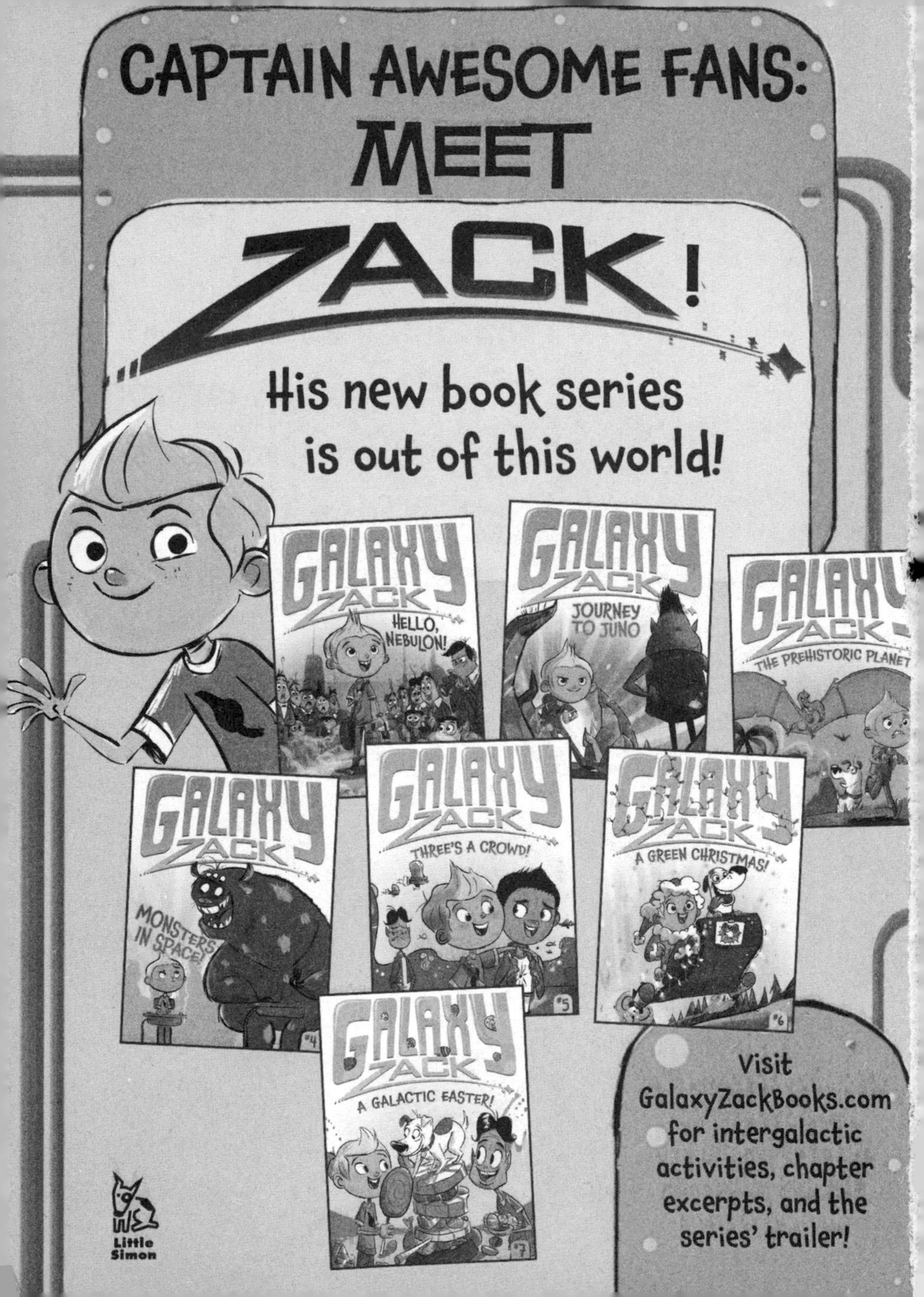
CAPTAIN AWESOME FANS:
MEET
ZACK!
His new book series is out of this world!
GALAXY ZACK
HELLO, NEBULON!
GALAXY ZACK
JOURNEY TO JUNO
GALAXY ZACK
THE PREHISTORIC PLANET
GALAXY ZACK
MONSTERS IN SPACE!
#4
GALAXY ZACK
THREE'S A CROWD!
#5
GALAXY ZACK
A GREEN CHRISTMAS!
#6
GALAXY ZACK
A GALACTIC EASTER!
#7
Visit GalaxyZackBooks.com for intergalactic activities, chapter excerpts, and the series' trailer!
Little Simon